The Forest Railway Stories

Teddy's Christmas

Book
2

Written & Illustrated by Matt Crossfield

Published by LIGHTMOOR PRESS

© Lightmoor Press & Matt Crossfield 2019

British Library Cataloguing-in-Publication Data. A catalogue record for this book is available from the British Library

ISBN: 9781911038 70 2

LIGHTMOOR PRESS

Unit 144B, Harbour Road Trading Estate,
Lydney, Gloucestershire GL15 4EJ
www.lightmoor.co.uk
info@lightmoor.co.uk

Lightmoor Press is an imprint of Black Dwarf Lightmoor Publications Ltd

Printed in Poland.
www.lfbookservices.co.uk

Permission to use the representation of 'Teddy' diesel No. D9555 in this book kindly given by the owner of the locomotive, Rob Staines.

Permission to use representations of locomotives No. 5541 and No. 9681 in this book kindly given by the Dean Forest Locomotive Group CIO. Charity No. 1164847.

This book belongs to . . . .

If you ever visit the Forest Railway,
where the trains are so helpful and friendly.

You might meet a green diesel engine,
who goes by the name of Teddy.

Teddy's job was to help haul trucks up and down the Forest Railway. One day, as Autumn came, he saw some moles digging in a nearby field.

Suddenly a mole peaked up from the tracks.
"Beg pardon," apologised the mole,
"I hope you don't mind!"

D9555

The mole said no more and went back to the field.

And Teddy rattled away.

'Clank!' 'Clank!'

As the leaves left the trees, Winter came.
Snow fell across the forest,
covering fields and the entire railway.

"I don't like it," said Driver Dusty Dave.

"Snow's trouble and it's hard to get through in this weather."

Even in the bitter fields, the busy moles carried on digging in the snow.

Teddy looked on whilst waiting at a signal and scoffed.

"I run on diesel oil" he boasted,

"So why would I ever be grateful for them?"

"Don't be so rude" said his driver.
"They work very hard, and you never know,
you might need their help one day."

"Pooh!" snorted the green diesel engine snootily.

Soon Christmas came and the streets were filled with lights and decorations.

Beautiful Christmas trees lit up homes, and everyone gathered presents for a very special night.

The railway always ran a very festive train and on board was the jolliest person ever:

Santa Claus!

With his helpful elves and sacks of toys,
he delivered Christmas charm to every girl and boy.

One particular day, Santa was stuck at Parkend station and Teddy had
to pick him up.

Although he chugged carefully through the glistening white forest, he was still arrogant.

"Silly moles! Silly snow!" he mumbled to himself.

Suddenly, around the bend was

"BO

OF!"

...a huge bank of snow.
Teddy was dazed and surprised,
he couldn't move forwards or backwards.

He was feeling very sorry for himself.

"Oh dear oh dear!" grumbled the green engine.
"I'll have to stay here all day."

Driver Dusty Dave then had a thought,

"You know...

"...We could ask the moles! After all
it's what they are good at, digging!"

Teddy never felt more relieved to see
the moles as they got to work.

'Dig!'

Soon Teddy was free from the snow,
and was very grateful for the moles' help.

'Beep!

He roared back into action and made his way to Parkend station to pick up Santa and his little elves.

Soon a very merry Santa was on board
the special train, giving presents to cherish and
share to every excited child. As he pulled the
festive train up and down the line,

Teddy already knew what he was thankful for.

"They are helpful really, I suppose."

Meet the Moles!

FOREST FREE MINERS

The Moles are following a long tradition of Free Mining in the Forest of Dean. Someone who was born and is living in the Forest of Dean, and who has worked for a year and a day in a Forest mine, has the right to claim a mine or 'gale' of their own. They pay a royalty on the minerals raised, which could be coal, iron ore or stone. There are thought to be around 30 Free Miners still working in the Forest of Dean today, keeping this ancient right alive.

How many Robins have you
found in this book? Clue:
There isn't one on every page!

Also, have you seen Rudolf?
He is hiding somewhere!

About the Author

Matt Crossfield is a young author and illustrator, who graduated from the University of South Wales, Cardiff, with a BA Hons in Animation.

He was the winner of the Young Cartoonist of the Year Award 2018, a national competition organised by the British Cartoonist Association. Matt is also very pleased and excited to have been chosen to design the 2019 Christmas cards for The Prince's Trust.

This is the second book in the Forest Railway Stories series, the first being about the Sheep Family in the Forest of Dean. Railways have always been one of his interests and Matt has been a volunteer on the Dean Forest Railway at Norchard for some time.

Matt says: "I hope you've enjoyed reading these books as much as I've enjoyed writing about Teddy and all the Forest Railway characters. Wishing you a very happy Christmas and see you soon for more adventures!"

Matt with his sales and display stand at Toddington on the Gloucestershire Warwickshire Railway. To see more of Matt's work visit his website:
www.mattcrossfield.com

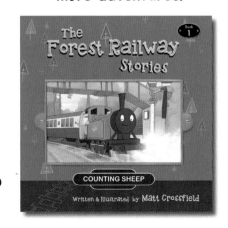

The Forest Railway Stories 1: Counting Sheep

40 pages, card cover, ISBN: 9781911038 54 2. Price £5